TO:

_____

FROM:

_____

DATE:

_____

hello, little Dreamer

BY KATHIE LEE GIFFORD

ILLUSTRATED BY ANITA SCHMIDT

Tommy NELSON

An Imprint of Thomas Nelson

Hello, Little Dreamer

© 2020 Kathie Lee Gifford

Tommy Nelson, PO Box 141000, Nashville, TN 37214

Published in Nashville, Tennessee, by Tommy Nelson. Tommy Nelson is an imprint of Thomas Nelson. Thomas Nelson is a registered trademark of HarperCollins Christian Publishing, Inc.

Tommy Nelson titles may be purchased in bulk for educational, business, fund-raising, or sales promotional use. For information, please e-mail SpecialMarkets@ ThomasNelson.com.

Scripture quotations are from the Tree of Life (TLV) Translation of the Bible. Copyright © 2015 by The Messianic Jewish Family Bible Society.

ISBN 978-1-4002-2614-6 (B&N)
ISBN 978-1-4002-2612-2 (BAM)
ISBN 978-1-4002-0927-9 (board book)
ISBN 978-1-4002-1063-3 (eBook)

Library of Congress Cataloging-in-Publication Data
Names: Gifford, Kathie Lee, 1953-author. | Schmidt, Anita (Illustrator), illustrator.
Title: Hello, little dreamer / Kathie Lee Gifford; illustrated by Anita Schmidt.
Description: Nashville, Tennessee: Thomas Nelson, [2020] | Audience: Ages 4–8. |
    Summary: Illustrations and rhyming text convey the message that God plants
    dreams in each individual, and wants every dream He gave to come true.
Identifiers: LCCN 2020004634 (print) | LCCN 2020004635 (ebook) | ISBN
    9781400209262 (hardcover) | ISBN 9781400209279 (board) | ISBN 9781400210633
    (epub)
Subjects: CYAC: Stories in rhyme—Fiction. | Individuality—Fiction. | God
    (Christianity)—Love—Fiction. | Christian life—Fiction.
Classification: LCC PZ8.3.G3723 Hel 2020 (print) | LCC PZ8.3.G3723 (ebook) | DDC [E]—
    dc23
LC record available at https://lccn.loc.gov/2020004634
LC ebook record available at https://lccn.loc.gov/2020004635
ISBN 978–1–4002–0926–2

Illustrated by Anita Schmidt

Printed in China
20 21 22 23 24 DSC 10 9 8 7 6 5 4 3 2 1
Mfr: DSC / Dongguan, China / September 2020 / PO #9589862

"Let the little children come to Me!
Do not hinder them, for the kingdom
of God belongs to such as these."

—Mark 10:14 TLV

Hello, little dreamer!

What is your **FAVORITE** thing to do?

Do you like to sing songs or watch **ANIMALS** at the zoo?

Do you like to **COUNT** numbers or **GAZE** at stars in the sky?

You may know what you like, but do you really know **WHY?**

Well, the answer is SIMPLE; it began long ago.
Before you were born, your dreams started to grow.

God planted these dreams way down deep in your HEART—
Some big and some little, right from the start.

And He had a good reason to do this, you see.

It's so you could become all

that you're MEANT TO BE.

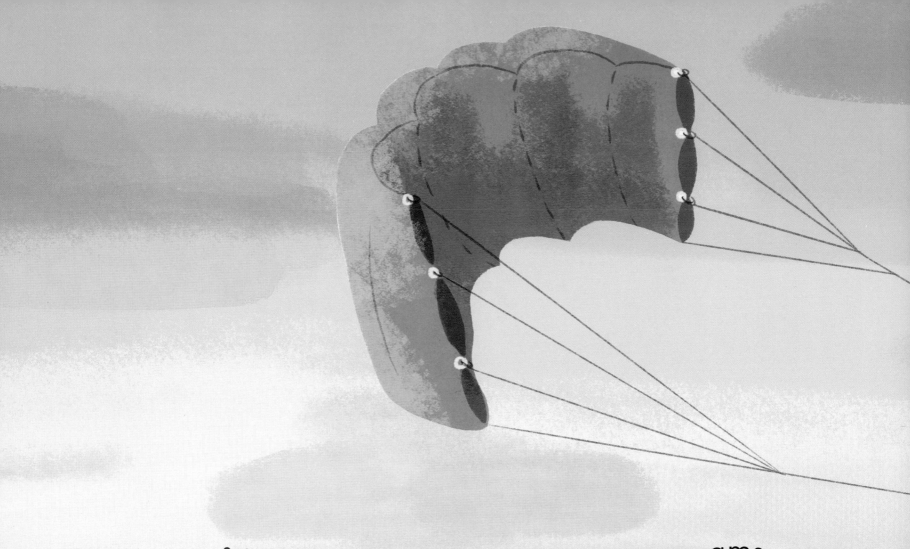

And the **wonderful** thing we know about dreams

Is a dream isn't always

exactly what it **seems**.

One dream may **come true** before you even know it,
While one might take longer 'cause God has to grow it.

Think of an acorn—it starts out so small,
Until many years later it's a tree,

STRONG AND TALL.

Well, that's just like you
when you are a **baby**.
You grow more each day,
until some day, just maybe . . .

Wow! There you are!
You're taller than your dad!

You didn't feel it happen, but now you're **so glad!**

And doesn't it make you happy

when you try something NEW,

And it becomes that one thing

that you JUST LOVE to do?

That's because it's a **DREAM** that God put deep inside!

Some dreams show up fast while some seem to hide.

And those deep hidden dreams may take years to come true,

Like a painting God paints until **YOU** become **YOU!**

This was God's **plan**.
This was what He designed
Because right from the start
He had you on His mind!
He wanted every child to know
His love and His joy,

So He planted **good dreams**

in each girl and each boy.

All children are different, and all dreams are too.

If we were all the same, you wouldn't be you!

So **THANK** the good Lord for the time that He takes

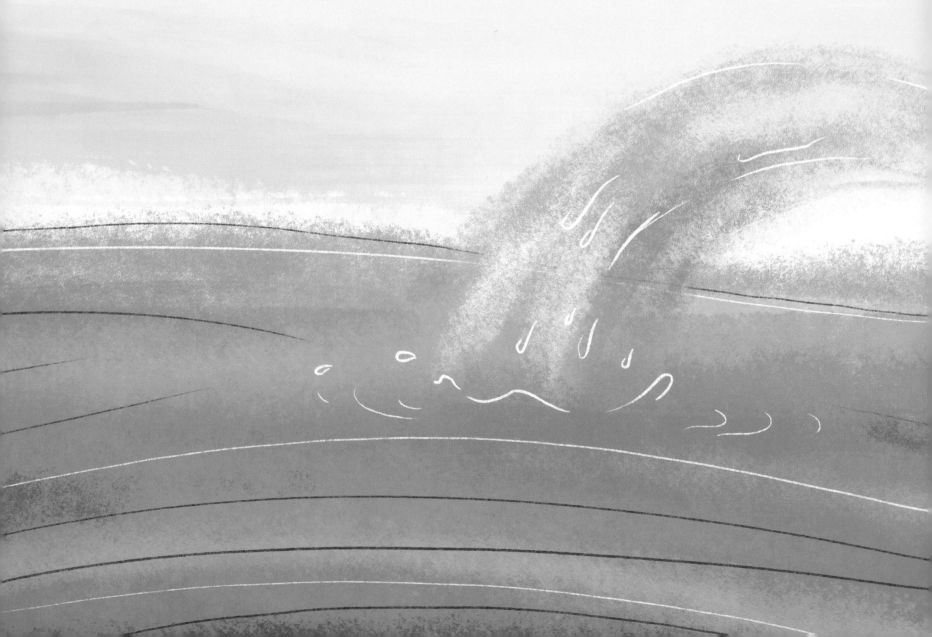

To put those SWEET DREAMS

in each person He makes.

NEVER let people tell you your dreams can't come true. Just keep doing those things that God wants you to do.

Keep believing and trusting Him more every day.

Give thanks for His **BLESSINGS** and remember to pray.

For God hears your prayers, and He's a *dreamer* too!

And He wants every dream He ever gave you *to come true.*